a minedition book *published by Penguin Young Readers Group*

Coproduction with Michael Neugebauer Publishing Ltd., Hong Kong.
Rights arranged with "minedition" Rights and Licensing AG, Zurich, Switzerland.

Published simultaneously in Canada.
Manufactured in Hong Kong by Wide World Ltd.
Typesetting in Sabon

Library of Congress Cataloging-in-Publication Data available upon request.
ISBN 0-698-40039-9
10 9 8 7 6 5 4 3 2 1
First Impression

For more information please visit our website: www.minedition.com

Chloe and the Magic Baton

Told and illustrated by Julie Litty
English translation by Charise Myngheer

Chloe rode to the stall as fast as her legs could pedal.
Today's competition was important, and she needed
to be on time.
Chloe could already hear the ponies whinnying
and shuffling their hoofs.
Everyone was getting prepared, and
the excitement was contagious.
"I wonder which horse I
will be riding today?"
thought Chloe nervously.
She knew the right horse
could make all the difference.

When Chloe saw the riding list, she couldn't believe it. "No!" she cried. "This can't be!" Today, Chloe would be riding Niki.

Niki was one of the most beautiful ponies in the region. But he was best known for his thick head. He never followed the rider's commands. "How can I depend on such a stubborn pony?" Chloe thought.

Chloe didn't want anyone to realize her disappointment, so she tried to smile as she led Niki out of the stable.

But as soon as Anna saw her, she commented immediately. "What? You have to ride that donkey!" Anna said. "You poor thing. You have no chance of winning now."

Unfortunately, Anna was right. Chloe had been working on her riding skills every day after school. She was comfortable with every horse... every horse except Niki. He seemed to have a mind of his own.
"Better luck next time," thought Chloe, disappointed.

She thought about talking to her coach, but there wasn't enough time. Chloe brushed Niki without saying a word. By the time she had him saddled up, she felt like she was going to cry.

Just when Chloe thought that things couldn't get worse, she turned around and saw her Uncle Tony standing there.
He'd never seen her cry.
"What's wrong?" he asked.
"Just everything!" answered Chloe. Then, she explained.
Uncle Tony smiled and said, "Chloe, this is your lucky day! Everything is going to be okay. I brought you a special present – all the way from Mexico – and it's magical."
Chloe stared in disbelief as he handed it to her.
"What could it be?" she wondered.
Quickly, Chloe opened it.

It was a riding baton!
But it wasn't an ordinary, everyday riding baton.
It was the most beautiful baton Chloe had ever seen.
She was so anxious to try it out that she forgot about her problems.
"The competition is about to begin," her Uncle said, nodding his head and smiling at her. "Thanks, Uncle Tony!" Chloe said, taking a firm hold of Niki's reign and leading him to the start.

As the bell sounded, Chloe bent down and whispered into Niki's ear. "It's time to show the others what we've got!" "Come on," Chloe said. "Our baton is magical. We can win!" Chloe hoped he understood as she gave him a little nudge with her heels.

Niki's start was a little slow, but at least he was moving.
Niki began to pick his hoofs up a little higher. The rhythm of his gallop became easier for Chloe to manage, and his speed gradually increased. They approached their first jump. Chloe held on tight. Wow! Niki sprang over the obstacle as if he knew how to fly! Now they had everyone's attention, especially Anna's. One jump after the other, Niki's performance was perfect.

"Unbelievable!" shouted someone from the crowd.
Chloe's friends gathered around.
She bent down and stroked Niki's neck.
"My uncle was right," she said.
"This baton really is magical!"

From that moment on, Chloe, Niki, and the colorful baton were inseparable. They rode together from one victory to the next.

Finally, the biggest competition of the season was before them. It had been a long time coming, and all of Chloe's hard work had been in preparation for this moment. Everyone had come to watch, including Uncle Tony.

Chloe brushed Niki and saddled him up. She reached into her bag for her baton, but it wasn't there.

Chloe searched everywhere, but
the colorful baton had disappeared.

Not knowing what else to do, Chloe left the stall, guiding Niki into the woods.
"Without the baton, we don't have a chance of winning," Chloe said to Niki. "No chance at all!"
"We're not going back," she decided. "We've come too far to embarrass ourselves now."

The announcer called for the next riders.
"Numbers 30, 31 and 32, please come to the start," he announced. Number 32 was Chloe's number, but she didn't stop. Tears began to run down her cheeks. Then suddenly, Niki planted his hoofs firmly in the ground. He turned around and began moving in the opposite direction.
"Stop!" commanded Chloe. "Where are you going? Stay!" she called again. But Niki didn't listen.

Against her will, Chloe soon found herself at the starting gate.
The judges nodded that they were ready.

Chloe looked around at her friends and family.
"This is terrible," she thought. "I'm going to disappoint everyone."
"What's wrong with Chloe?" asked Anna. "Why does she look so strange?"
"I have no idea," answered Uncle Tony.
Everyone watched with anticipation.
As the bell sounded, Chloe looked bewildered.

Niki's start was strong. He picked his hoofs up high and moved like a pro.
Chloe's start was a little weak. Then she began to sit up a little straighter.
The rhythm of her ride became easier to manage, and Niki's speed gradually increased.
Chloe realized that Niki believed in her. As they approached their first jump,
Chloe said, "Hold on!" She wasn't afraid of losing anymore.
Wow! They sprang over the obstacle as if they knew how to fly!
One jump after the other, their performance was perfect.

"Winner!" shouted Uncle Tony almost louder than the announcer.

As Chloe hugged Niki, she whispered, "You knew we could do it all the time, didn't you? That was all the magic we ever needed!"